For RCA

"Reflecting the moon's

gentle show,

and moonbeams glow

those who know,

Dreams of fantasy

and reality,

has no boundary. "

---

jca

For Riz & Riana
my blessings from heaven.

---

jca

THE
SECRET PASSAGE

JC ASUNCION

Hello,

My name is Janca

Janca Faerie
is a fictional character.

This is a fiction story
for young readers.

THE
SECRET PASSAGE

CONTENT

I.cottage

2.garden

3.passage

4.flowers

5.cave

6.light

7.home

8.poetry

Cottage

It's summer!

Janca is spending her vacation at her grandma's cottage in Northern Philippines. It's been three long years since she last visited her grandmother.

Her long and wavy brunette hair sways as she jumps happily. She stands about one hundred 63 centimetres. Her eyes have distinct colours of deep brown at her right eye and a mixture of purple and brown on her left eye.

Janca is so excited that she could ride her pink bike and play in the garden like she used to do. She also planned to make a new tik-tok dance and upload video reels on her instagram.

" This place is gonna be awesome." she thought to herself. While excitedly unpacking her colorful clothes from her purple anello bag.

She hums a little as she looks at her mobile phone. " I3% battery charge.Where's my charger?"

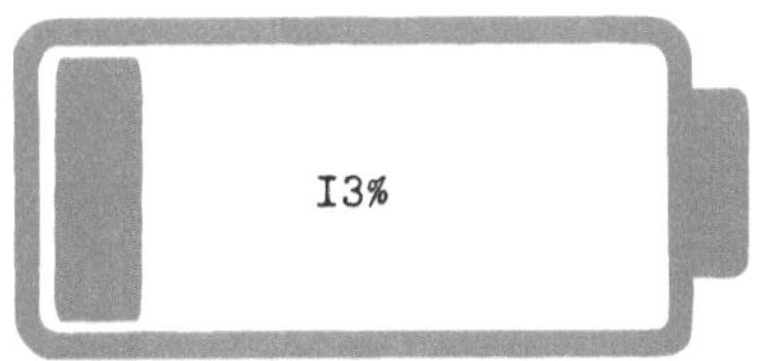

She pulled the sparky pink
pouch and took the black
cord.

"Yes, the charger is here!"
she whispred, she felt proud
of herself, that she didn't
forget to bring her own
charger.

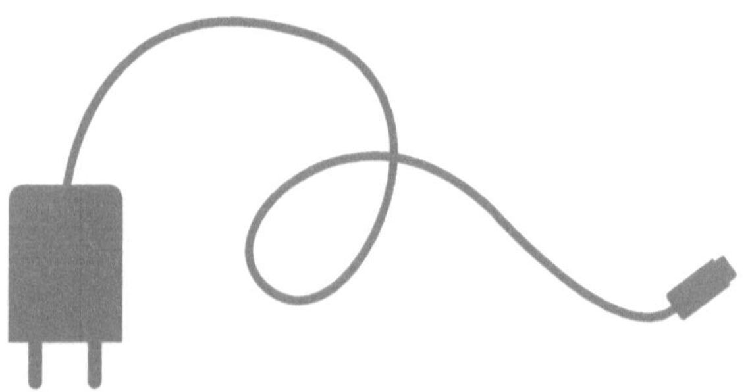

"Janca it's three o'clock,
snacks are ready" her
grandmother said.

Her nose are very happy that
she can smell the freshly
baked muffins.

"Oh! My favorites banana
muffins with dark chocolate
bits" and she kissed and
gaveher grandmother a tight
hug.

"Salamat - for being here"
grandma uttered. This is how
her grandmother says Thank
You in tagolog, one of the
Philippines famous dialect.

"Thank you grandma .I miss
being here" Janca said while
merrily chewing a muffin
like a winner.

"Yum! I missed this muffins"
as she gobbled the flavourful
muffins immediately because
her stomach is already
growling in hunger.

Grandma's old cottage stood amidst a picturesque countryside, emanating an air of rustic charm. Its pristine white exterior, a little weathered by the time, contrasted beautifully with the lush greenery that surrounded. The cottage stood low to the ground, boasting it's charm and simplicity creating an enchanting scenery.

As one approached the cottage, they would notice the hand curved detailsthat added to its character.Time-worn wooden shatters adorned the windows, painted in a soft shade of faded blue.Giving a touch of whimsy to
its facade. A picket fence enclosed the cottage , its edges adorned with blossoming peonies and wild roses.Their fragrance embracing the air with delicate sweetness.

"Yes, this is it, my first video background " Janca said. A video-reels update for her friend as she delightedly set up the camera.

Garden

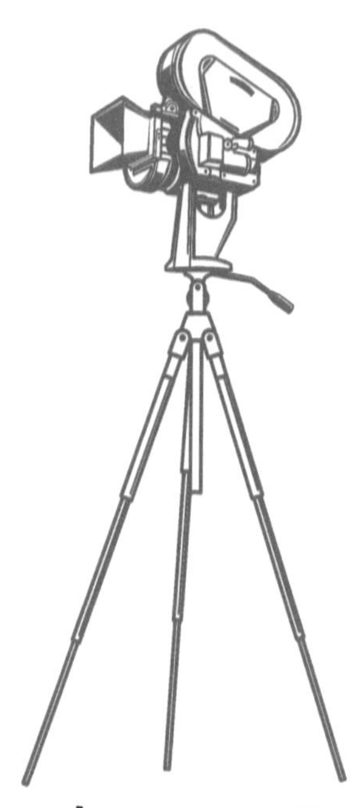

"Hi guys! Janca here, welcome to my world! I'm at my grandma's where adventure awaits. Join me as I explore the hidden gems and incedible beauty of the place." She gleefully announced as she recorded a video of herself.

She moved her hand to focus the
camera at the butterfly. Janca
curiously followed the tiny
fluttering purple butterfly,
who kissed her left cheek and
hide behind the bushes.

"Where are you going pretty
butterfly? Give me a nice shot"
Janca said.

The butterfly fluttered its
wings and gracefully entered a
small door. The passage became
bigger in size as Janca pushed
on brass the handle ,polished
to mirror like shine. Where she
could see her pale curious face
reflection.

"Where does this secret passage
leads to?" she thought to
herself while blinking trice
making sure of herself that she
is not dreaming.

Passage

As Janca slowly opens the passage,she quietly walks through pathway of shiny stones, slightly covered with a foliage. The beautiful leaves in colours of golden crisp and reddish brown.The seating area was made of woods and precious stones. Adorned with soft thick cushions in pastel colours of baby pink, periwinkle, and lavender. A nice corner that could invite everyone to enjoy a relaxing afternoon tea. A delicious snack was prepared at the center of the garden.

The aromatic scent of roses
and peonies fills the warm
summer air. Bees were busy
buzzing like, singing
around the various flowers,
while gathering pollen and
nectar to bring back to
their hive. A mesmerizing
scenario, that looks like
in a fantasy film perhaps a
like a magical fairlytale.

Golden fountains and bird
baths were in the middle
part of the mystical garden.
Adding a charm of
chandeliers and wind chaims
hanging on the arc roses
vines. The assorted colour
of butterflies were flying
to meet and gladly meet her.
 " Welcome, Janca "

She approached a flower bush
with a dark blueish green
leaves in full blooms in
shades of pink , red, white,
and purple. She cannot
resist touching the big
petals of a purple flowers ,
they were so beautiful to
unnoticed.

Flowers

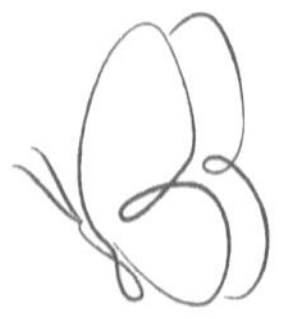

To her surprised, a tiny
creature popped up from the
thick flowers, with
charming iridescent purple
wings like a butterfly and
pretty face pointy eyes
just like her grandma used
to describe on her bedtime
stories.

"Hello Janca , it's been a
while,"
the delicate fairy greeted
her
 with a tiny, clear voice.

The stunning sight of the
garden and a fairy at the
same time gave Janca the
overwhelming gladness to
see it all at once. A fairy
who looks familiar but
could not really recall
her. It was a moment of
nostalgic and magical at
the same time.

"Oh, pretty, are you real?
You know my name? What's
your name?" She was
uttering too many words.

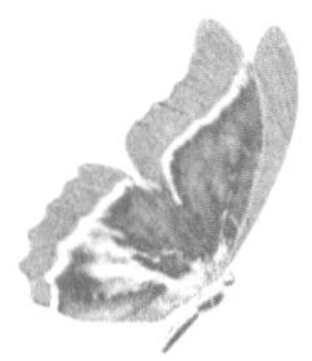

The glowing butterflies
guided her to the shining
light that caught her
attention. The sound soft
of tingling bells and the
gentle movement of each
flower opened slowly to
show the seven baby fairies
sleeping peacefully. The
thick flower bushes are the
baby fairies cradle.

Janca standing still
mesmerised, staring to the
mystical beauty of the
place and watching the
magnificently fluttering
fairies.

"Butterflies could be
fairies, too" Janca thought

She started to look for her way back home, as she could hear grandma's voice calling her. Panic on her face begins to make her heart beat so fast lika drum off rowing boat festival as she can see her surroundings starting to shake and fall apart like an earthquake with strong intensity. The beautiful enchanted garden is beginning to disappear. Janca is crying. " Please stop , don't go."

Cave

She started to look for her way back home, as she could hear grandma's voice calling her. Panic on her face begins to make her heart beat so fast like a fast drum that is loud

She can see her surroundings starting to shake like an earthquake with strong intensity. The beautiful enchanted garden is beginning to disappear. Janca is crying. " Please stop , don't go."

Everything became black and silence ate the whole place I cannot see anything. A cold air fills her lungs, and a strange feeling creeps up on her spine. The silence is broken only by the sound of water droplets echoing somewhere, and it all feels chilly ominous.

Strange noises can be heard in a distance not so far.Rumbling, scurrying, and fluttering tiny wings. Janca 's heart begins to race again and can feel something or someone is lurking in the darkness. She hugged herself so tight and prayed.

Light

"Janca here,"
"This way! " the gnome
noting to the light at end
of the cave.

Janca saw a tiny shimmering
purple butterfly and a
small familiar face,
smiling at her.

"Janca this way, let's go,"
he said again.

Namby, her childhood friend
Gnome is here to help. All
those years, Janca thought
that Namby was just an
imaginary friend.

"Janca you must leave
before the cave closes."
Namby said as the purple
butterfly twitched its
wings moving forward to
Janca's hand leading her to
the secret passage.

She opened her eyes and saw the rock formations around are jagged and twisted, casting eerie, distortedshadow. She could smell a faint musty in the air and slipperry rocks beneath her feet. This path could make her slip anytime if she moves without knowing her way out. Stalactites and stalagmites are like daggers pointed at her.

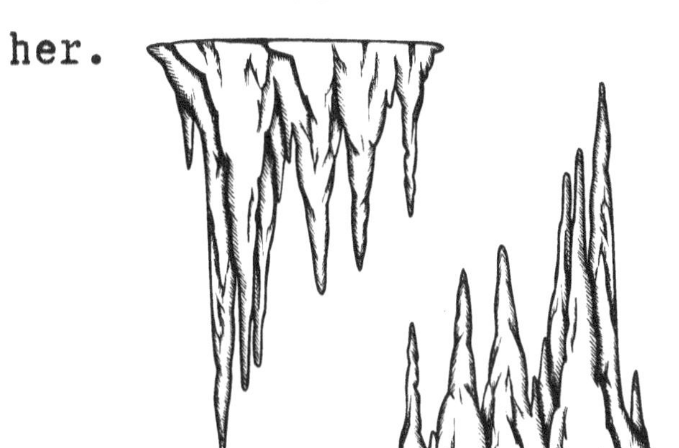

She ran so fast while
carrying Namby and
following the butterfly as
she was guided to the cave
exit. The cave is moving
like it's shrinking, and
darkness is creeping all
over again. Janca was so
determined to escape the
dark cave. She moved so
quickly and saw the bright.
She tried to open her eyes
but could not move. There
is something stopping her,
something heavy on her
other hand.

Home

Janca is too tired. All she
wanted was to go home. Home
is an indescribable feeling
that awakens her sense of
comfort and belongingness.
It's the sound of familiar
laughters and feelings of
peacefulness that evoke
security. And as she think
about going home, it gave her
a courage to move quicker .

Janca wake up,
Why are you sleeping with
the sheers? We don't have
to cut the thick bushes,
just the grass, dear"
Grandma shouted from the
window cottage

Slowly Janca opened her
eyes and saw grandma's
cats. At her left side a
grey cat is licking her
face like an ice cream
while the ginger cat is
playing with the butterfly.

She got up and ran towards
the bushes near the oak
tree and gazed at the
charming flowers and
glimmering butterflies.

The purple butterfly
transforms into flying
fairy, time seemed to stand
still, as the world below
disappeared into a blur of
colours and shapes. With
every graceful movement and
mischievous grin, she
brought a touch of magic to
ordinary moments, reminding
all who witnessed her
flight that there is a
world beyond what human
eyes can

see - a world of wonder,
where dreams take flight and
the extraordinary becomes
reality.

  The fairy says,
" Thank you, Janca for not
destroying our home." And she
blew a kiss on the air.

Before Janca could say a
single word, the fairy was
already gone and left some
sparking dust on the air as
Namby waving goodbye to her.

~ Garden ~

Pretty garden
an enchanting retreat
Where hearts find solace
dreams find a seat
Paper,ink and magic
mix and blend
imagination knows
no end.

-jc asuncion

~Dream~

Where dreams take shape
and light shines,
Lies a mystical garden
hidden from afar.
Where enchantment blooms,
vibrant and true
All is seen in a dreamers
of a dream.

-jc asuncion

~Fantasy~

Reflecting the moon's
gentle glow,
Casting a spell in all
those who know,
dream of fantasy
and reality,
it has no boundary.

-jc asuncion

About the Author

JC ASUNCION

a frelance writer,TEFL graduate,
who loves to take random
photos on her budget trips.
She believes that kindness should
be sprinkled anywhere we go.

Other Books

The Lost Girl

Coming soon:

Janca Faerie: Jaunt in Singapore

janca faerie collection